Once they were out of their clothes, Cordy lay on the bed and María stretched out on top of her.

"This is how you like it," María said with a smile. Her long black hair was a mass of curls around her head. She was a strikingly beautiful woman, and Cordy felt lucky to be a part of her life.

"I like the way you remember that," Cordy said as she reached up and moved a spray of dark curls from María's eyes. "Yes," she whispered. "This is how I like it." She arched her back and rubbed her breasts into María's. "Who wouldn't like this?" Cordy asked before she kissed her again.

Visit

Bella Books

at

BellaBooks.com

or call our toll-free number
1-800-729-4992